## This Book Belongs To:

..............................................................................................

*Illustrated by Caroline Pedler*
*Retold by Gaby Goldsack*

Marks and Spencer p.l.c.
PO Box 3339
Chester CH99 9QS

shop online
www.marksandspencer.com

ISBN 978-1-84805-791-3
Printed in China

# The Nutcracker

MARKS &
SPENCER

One cold and frosty Christmas Eve night,
the Stahlbaum house shone festive and bright.
Twinkling candles lit up the tree
as guests arrived for the Stahlbaums' party.
Clara and Fritz both clapped to see treats
of chocolates, candy canes, sugar mice and sweets.

The last to arrive was Herr Drosselmeyer,
who offered his gifts for all to admire.
Clara and Fritz chuckled and cheered,
as two life-size dolls suddenly appeared.
Then Clara and Fritz watched with delight,
as the magical dolls danced in the twilight.

Then Herr Drosselmeyer, the children's godfather,
gave a splendid Nutcracker doll to Clara.
In his smart uniform he stood proud and tall –
the very finest gift of them all.
But before Clara's thanks had even been spoken,
Fritz grabbed the doll and it was broken!

Herr Drosselmeyer, being kindly and good,
tried mending the Nutcracker's splintered wood.
Then after much feasting, dancing and play,
Herr Drosselmeyer left on his sleigh.
As they waved goodnight, Clara's mother said,
"Hurry now, children, it's time for bed."

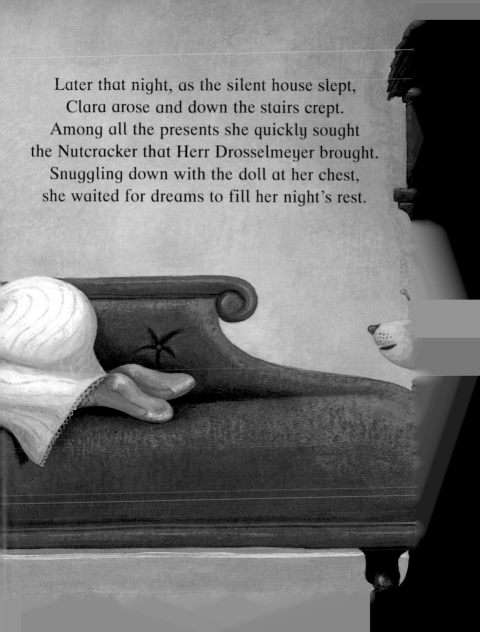

Later that night, as the silent house slept,
Clara arose and down the stairs crept.
Among all the presents she quickly sought
the Nutcracker that Herr Drosselmeyer brought.
Snuggling down with the doll at her chest,
she waited for dreams to fill her night's rest.

Before very long she awoke with a fright,
startled by strange sounds in the still night.
Sitting up quickly and blinking her eyes,
she saw that the toys had grown to life size!
Her beloved Nutcracker stood mighty and tall,
so that, when she stood by him, Clara felt small.

Behind him tin soldiers stood in a row
with their muskets all loaded and ready to go.
Then a troop of grey mice marched into the room
and started a battle by the light of the moon.
The mighty mouse army, led by the Mouse King,
bombarded the soldiers and looked set to win.

The Nutcracker commanded as best he could,
but they were outnumbered – it didn't look good.
When the Nutcracker fell, Clara took up her shoe,
and aimed at the Mouse King, then desperately threw.
The soldiers all cheered as the King was struck down.
The mice were defeated and the toys seized his crown.

When Clara looked into the Nutcracker's eyes
she was amazed, and gasped with surprise.
For during the battle, or perhaps even since,
he had changed from a doll to a handsome young prince!
Now the prince looked at Clara, bowed down and cried,
"Come, my dear Clara, let's go outside!"

The prince led Clara to a magical sleigh
that flew through the night to a land far away.
There, beneath the stars twinkling bright,
enchanted snowflakes danced through the night.
"The dance is for you," the handsome prince said.
"But we mustn't stop here, there's more fun ahead."

They journeyed on to the Kingdom of Sweets,
a land full of dancing and sugary treats.
The Sugar Plum Fairy, so dainty and nice,
danced especially for Clara on a stage of ice.
Next came a dance from the sweets of the world,
who made Clara dizzy as they twisted and twirled.

The next thing she knew, Clara was awoken
and her Nutcracker doll was no longer broken.
Had her adventure been all that it seemed,
or was it a fantasy she had just dreamed?
But Clara's questions were soon chased away
as Fritz wished her a Merry Christmas Day!